BEAR

American Indian Legends Retold by E. K. Caldwell
Additional Text & Book Design by Vic Warren
Illustrations by Diana Magnuson

SCHOLASTIC INC.
New York Toronto London Auckland Sydney

The tradition of American Indian storytelling is older than history. The authors are proud to bring this art form to the pages of this book, in the hope that we may entertain, educate, and inspire a new generation of children.

We wish to extend our special thanks to the Abenaki nation for giving us their kind permission to retell *The Good Bear and the Lost Boy*. We also wish to thank the Seneca and other Iroquois nations and the Passamaquoddy, Creek and Cherokee nations for their stories.

Additional thanks are due D. L. Birchfield for his technical assistance; Joseph Bruchac for sharing his knowledge of Abenaki and Iroquois stories; and Special Collections, University of Washington Libraries, for the Edward Curtis photo (neg. #4087) of Bear's Belly.

Copyright © 1996 by Turning Heads, Inc.
All rights reserved. Published by Scholastic Inc.

Library of Congress Cataloging-in-Publication Data

Caldwell, E. K.
    Animal lore & legend — bear / American Indian legends retold by E. K. Caldwell ; additional text & book design by Vic Warren ; illustrations by Diana Magnuson.
        p.   cm.
        Summary: Includes both factual information and Indian legends about North American bears.
    ISBN 0-590-22491-3
        1. Indians of North America — Folklore. 2. Bears —Folklore. 3. Bears — Juvenile literature. 4. Tales — North America. [1. Bears — Folklore. 2. Indians of North America — Folklore. 3. Bears.] I. Caldwell, E.K., 1954- . II. Warren, Vic, 1943- . III. Magnuson, Diana, ill., 1947- . IV. Title: Animal lore & legend — bear.
E98.F6A54 1995
398.24'52897'08997—dc20
          94-43935
          CIP
          AC

12 11 10 9 8 7 6 5 4 3 2 1   6 7 8 9/9 0 1/0

Printed in the U.S.A.   09

First Scholastic printing, January 1996

Photos:
Title page, Grizzly bear
Back cover, Black bear

E. K. Caldwell has roots in both North America and Europe. She is a Tsalagi/Shawnee/Celtic/German writer who lives and works on the Central Oregon Coast. Her poetry and short stories have appeared in various anthologies in the U.S. and Canada. Her work, *When The Animals Danced,* has been performed internationally. She also works as a journalist with the national Native newspaper, *News From Indian Country,* and for *The New York Times Syndicate*'s multicultural wire service. She is a member of the Native Writers' Circle of the Americas and serves on the National Advisory Caucus of Wordcraft Circle's Native Writers Program.

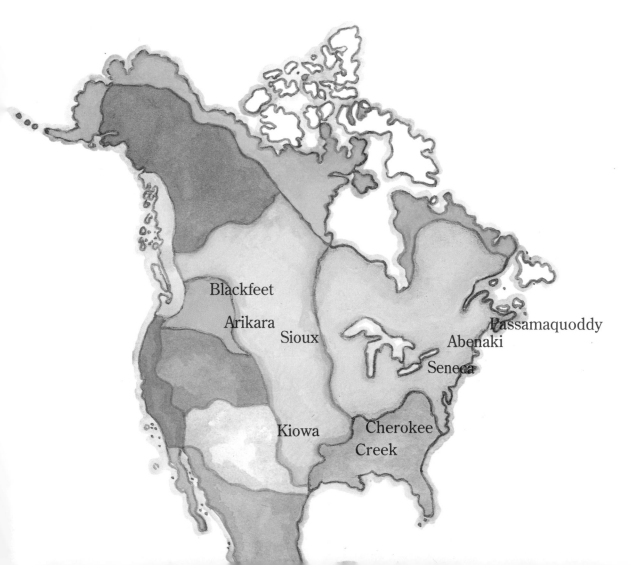

Blackfeet

Arikara

Sioux

Passamaquoddy

Abenaki

Seneca

Kiowa

Cherokee

Creek

Grizzly bear, polar bear, and black bear are the three kinds of bear that live in North America.

The grizzly bear is large and brown. Its thick fur is tipped with white. It has a humped back.

Grizzly bears have long, sharp claws. They are good for digging.

Polar bears live in the Arctic. They have heavy white fur. They have a thick layer of fat. They stay warm in the ice and snow.

The black bear is the smallest bear in North America. It lives both in the west and the east.

Black bears can be black or brown. Black bears have short claws that make them good tree climbers.

HOW BEAR LOST HIS TAIL

From the Seneca Story

Long ago, Bear and Fox were friends.
They played and rolled in the grass.
Bear was bigger, but Fox was smarter.
One thing they both had was long tails.

Flying Head was the wind's name.
He saw Bear and Fox playing.
He worried about Bear trusting Fox.
He came to talk to Bear.

"WHEO-who-eee-ooo-wee,"
said Flying Head to Bear.
"You better watch out.
Fox will trick you."

"Grr," said Bear.
"He will not trick me,
because we are friends."

"Yes, he woo-oo-will," said Flying Head.

One fall day Bear and Fox were playing.
They played so hard they got hungry.

"My belly is grrr-growling," said Bear.

"Let's find something to eat!" said Fox.

"You like berries?" asked Bear.

"Yuck! No way," said Fox.
"How about some muskrats?"

"Ick! I don't like muskrats," said Bear.
"What do we both like to eat?"

Fox got a big grin on his face.
"I know! I know! Let's go fishing!"

"Okay, fresh fish sounds good," said Bear.

And so off they went to the lake to fish.

They didn't have fishing poles
like people.

"Your tail is bigger than mine," said Fox.
"Use your tail to catch those fish!"

"Well, okay, I will," said Bear.

He swam out to a big stump in the lake.
He caught a lot of fish on his tail.
He threw them all to Fox.
And Fox ate every one of them himself!

WHOOSH! The wind started to blow
his cold breath.

Then the lake got still.
It looked like shiny glass.
Do you know why? Well, Bear didn't.

He felt a big bite on his tail.
This must be a monster fish,
he thought.
He tugged really hard, but no fish
came out.

Now Bear got scared.
It made him feel mad.
So he said, "One, two, I'll show you!"
And he pulled with all his might.

SNAP! went his tail, right into the lake!
And Bear went rolling across the ice.

Yes, you guessed it!
That lake was frozen solid!
It stole Bear's tail from him.
Boy, was he mad at Fox for tricking him.

Flying Head whistled,
"I told you so-whoo-ooo-oo!"

And to this day, bears have no tails.

Many Indians think bears are the animal most like humans. Many Indian stories tell of humans turning into bears.

Bears are known as healers. The Sioux watched bears dig up roots and eat herbs. They learned from the bear. Many of these roots and herbs cure sickness and ease pain.

Bears can stand on their back legs like humans.

Bears are omnivores like us. Omnivores eat all kinds of food. They like to eat meat and fish. They also like to eat berries, honey, moss, grass, leaves, roots, grubs, insects, nuts, and mushrooms.

Bears eat extra food in the fall. They sleep all winter in their dens. This is called hibernating.

A grizzly bear catches a salmon.

Bear's Belly, an Arikara shaman, in his sacred bear skin.

THE GOOD BEAR AND THE LOST BOY

From the Passamaquoddy and
Seneca Stories

Oskino was six years old.

He liked berries.

He picked berries with his people.

One day he saw a good berry patch.

He wandered off alone.

He saw a deep hole.

I wonder who lives there, he thought.

He leaned over as far as he could.

He lost his balance.

Crash! He fell down the dark hole.

He felt scared, and that made him cry.

He heard a voice say, "Come this way."
Two red eyes glowed in the darkness.
His heart beat faster, but he tried
to be brave.

He walked toward the red eyes.
They got BIGGER and BIGGER!

Then he saw it was kind old Porcupine.
"I will help you," said old Porcupine.
"Friends! Come, meet this boy!"

Oskino met Wolf, Raccoon, and Possum.
He met Robin, Beaver, and Turtle.
Oskino was happy to meet new friends.

Everyone wanted him to live with them.
But boys don't eat worms like Robin.
And boys don't eat bark like Beaver.

"Who can feed this boy?"
asked Porcupine.

Bear gave Oskino a flat blueberry cake.
The boy ate it and said, "Yum!"

Porcupine nodded wisely and smiled.
"Bear will be this boy's mother."

So Oskino went to live with the bears.
He had two bear cub brothers
and one sister.
They were all shy at first.

They showed Oskino how to be a bear.
They taught him to walk on all fours.
They showed him their secret places.

The bears became his family.
They loved Oskino.
Oskino loved them.

One morning they went fishing.
Mother Bear waded in and sat down.
Splash! She caught lots of smelt for
her children.

All at once she said, "Shhh! Listen!"
They heard footsteps. *Thud! Thud!*

"Who is it, Mama?" asked Oskino.

"Humans like you," said Mother Bear.

"Sometimes humans eat bears for food.
You must always run from humans."

When they got home, they all took a nap.
Oskino heard *Thud! Thud!* outside the den.
It was humans trying to get the bears!

"Mama, wake up, save us!"
cried Oskino.

"Oskino, only you can save us,"
said Mother Bear.
"Go out. They will see you are a boy."

Oskino was SO scared, but he went out.
"Wait! I am human!
These bears saved my life!"

"It is Oskino!
He is living with bears!" said a man.

"Listen to his story," said another man.
And they learned of his bear life.

"We won't hurt your bear family," said
the first man, "but you must come
home with us."

Mother Bear said, "Grr. He's right."

Oskino was sad to leave his bear family.
He got big bear hugs from them all.
He knew in his heart it was time to go.

He told them all he had a new name.
"My name is Muwinsis, the bear's son!
Bears are my family and my friends.
I will never harm any bears."

And Muwinsis kept his promise
his whole life.

Grizzly bear cubs

Baby bears are
called cubs.
They are born in
the winter.
They are tiny, bald,
and blind when
they are born.

Cubs stay in the
den all winter.
They feed on their
mother's rich milk.
Their fur grows
while the cubs are
in their den.

The cubs come out in the spring.
The mother bear teaches the cubs.
She shows them how to hunt.
She shows them what to eat.
She teaches them how to be safe.

Polar bear mother and cub

The cubs spend the winter with their
mother in a new den.
When they are two or three, they
leave to live on their own.

THE MOTHER BEAR'S SONG

From the Cherokee and Creek Stories

Once a man was walking in the woods.
He thought he heard a woman singing.
So he followed the sound to a cave.
He peeked in and saw a mother bear.
She was singing to her two bear cubs.
He hid so he could hear the song.

It was a lovely song.
The mother bear had a strong voice.

The song was about strangers.
The bear cubs listened closely.
Their mother was teaching them
how to be safe.

"Watch out for strangers," she sang.
"When you hear them coming from down
the creek, they will go *Splash! Splash!*
Then you must run away.
Upstream, upstream, you must go.

"If you hear them coming from up
the creek, they will go *Slosh! Slosh!*
Downstream, downstream, you must go.
Grr, grr. Then they can't hurt you.

"You might hear them walking
on dry leaves.
They will go *Crunch! Crunch!*
You must run away to the mountain.
Run away quickly.
Run away quietly.

"Late in the winter, right before spring,
we will wake from our winter dreams.
Then you might hear them walking
on hard snow.
They will go *Scrunch! Scrunch!*
Then you must run away.
Do not talk to human strangers.
Do not let them see you by yourself.
It is important to be safe."

The hiding man liked the song.
He went home to tell his children.

The bear cubs clapped their paws.

"It's a good song!" said the first cub.

"A song to remember!" said the second.

"If strangers come *Splash! Splash!*
from down the creek, we will run away.
Upstream, upstream, we will go.
If they *Slosh! Slosh!* from up the creek,
downstream, downstream, we will go.

"If they *Crunch! Crunch!* on dry leaves,
or *Scrunch! Scrunch!* on hard snow,
then to the high mountain we will go!"

Mother Bear was pleased with her cubs.
They learned because they listened.
She loved them.
She wanted them to be safe.
Someday, when they grew up,
they would sing this song to their cubs.

Grizzly bears once lived all
across western North America.
Now they are almost gone south
of Canada and Alaska.
They are an endangered species.
So are polar bears.
But there are still lots of
black bears.

The paw print of a bear is
much like a human footprint.
The Blackfeet word *o-kits-iks* means
both human hand and bear paw.

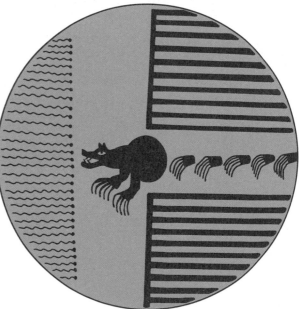

A bear charges bullets on
a Kiowa shield.

Sometimes bears seem cute and friendly.
Be careful if you see a bear.
All bears can be dangerous.

GLOSSARY

Abenaki (ob-a-nok´-ee): An Indian nation of the northern Atlantic Coast

Arikara (ar-ee-kar´-a): An Indian nation of the Great Plains

Blackfeet: An Indian nation of the northern Great Plains

Cherokee (chair´-o-kee): An Indian nation of southeastern North America

Creek: An Indian nation of southeastern North America

Endangered (in-dayn´-jurd): In danger; a word used for animals and plants that are almost extinct

Herb (urb): A plant used for medicine or for its smell or taste

Kiowa (ky´-oh-wah): An Indian nation of the Great Plains

Muwinsis: Passamaquoddy for "little bear"

Oskino: From the Abenaki word *ohskinnos*, which means "little boy"

Passamaquoddy: An Indian nation of the northern Atlantic Coast, the easternmost Abenaki nation

Seneca (sen´-a-ca): One of the six Iroquois nations of the Eastern Woodlands

Sioux (soo): An Indian nation of the Great Plains

Species (spee´-shees): A distinct kind of animal or plant